P9-CQX-669

There Will Be No Mouse In Grammy's House!

Happy Reading! ♡

Stephanie M. Wilkerson

10-5-2021

Stephanie M. Wilkerson

Copyright © 2020 Stephanie M. Wilkerson
All rights reserved
First Edition

Fulton Books, Inc.
Meadville, PA

Published by Fulton Books 2020

This book is based on actual event.

ISBN 978-1-64654-324-3 (hardcover)
ISBN 978-1-64654-323-6 (digital)

Printed in the United States of America

This book is lovingly dedicated
to
my four grandsons,
Ryan, Grayson, Brennan, and Landon,
who are my source of constant
inspiration!

My name is Sammy, and I have a fun Grammy! One day a week, she invites me to stay while Mommy and Daddy go out for the day. Since Grammy's house is a really cool place, you know why I have a big smile on my face.

Sometimes we play, or we read a good book, but one recent day, we decided to cook.

In the kitchen, you see just my Grammy and me were making our favorite recipe—chocolate chip cookies!

3

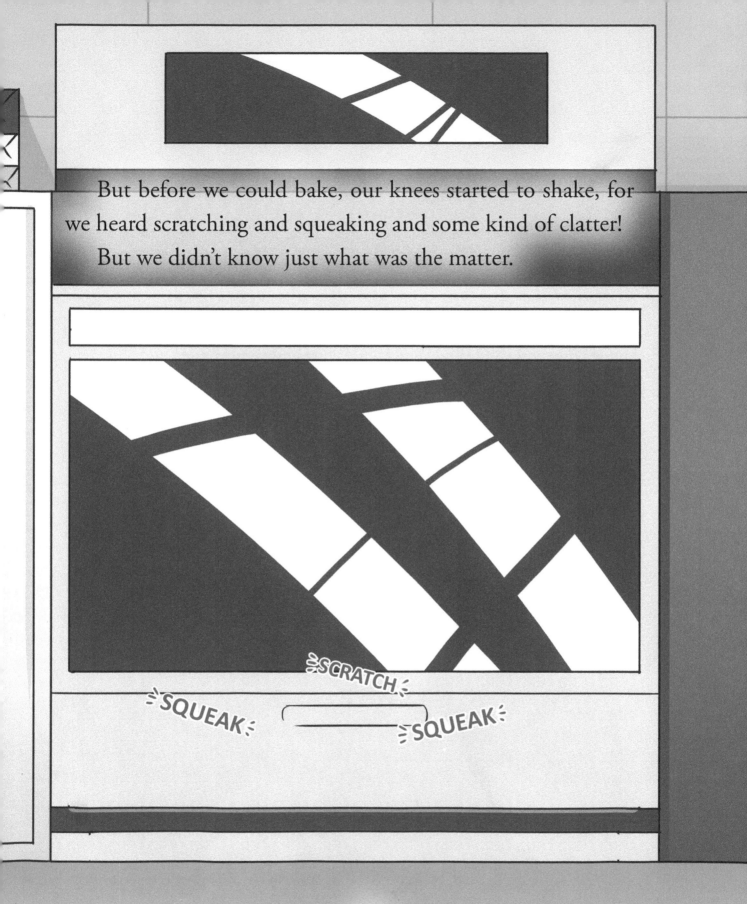

But before we could bake, our knees started to shake, for we heard scratching and squeaking and some kind of clatter! But we didn't know just what was the matter.

The noises came from down low and were strange, and they seemed to come from my Grammy's range.

So I opened the drawer, as brave as can be, and what do you think was peeking at me?

My Grammy was shrieking, but I was NOT.
"After all," I said, "It's just a mouse in a pot!"

But Grammy started running all through the house and just because of a little grey mouse!

Now we don't want to hurt you. Oh no, little guy, but Grammy's upset, and she's ready to cry! So I picked up the pot with the mouse still inside, but he scurried out because he wanted to hide.

All through the rooms, I chased him, you know. I wanted to keep him, but he had to go! Over and under, around and through, oh what tricks *this* mouse could do!

He sped over the mantel and set off the clock, making it chime, but when would it stop?

Round and round the table and chairs, then over the bookcase and down the front stairs.

Now Grammy was following. What a sight to be sure all three of us running right out the front door!

Into the yard, not far from the street, my goodness, this mouse had fast little feet!

And then as easy as one, two, three, that little mouse scampered right up our big tree. And he was gone…

Then I looked at Grammy; she looked at me, and we collapsed in a heap right under that tree, and we laughed and laughed and laughed ourselves silly.

Because when you have a fun Grammy, it doesn't matter what you do. You can play, read or cook, or chase a mouse too. You'll always have a really great time if you're lucky to have a Grammy like mine!

Now Grammy pretended to get very gruff, shook her finger at me, and said, "That's enough!"

But I saw the twinkle in her little eye, knew she was smiling, and thought I knew why because now...THERE WILL BE NO MOUSE IN GRAMMY'S HOUSE!

The End

About the Author

There Will Be No Mouse in Grammy's House is the first book for Stephanie M. Wilkerson, who has been writing stories and poems for children for over twelve years.

She has gotten many ideas and much inspiration from her four grandchildren.

Ms. Wilkerson, who is also a caregiver to the elderly in their homes, resides in Northern Baltimore County in Cockeysville, Maryland.

CPSIA information can be obtained
at www.ICGtesting.com
Printed in the USA
BVHW020947250821
614731BV00007B/11

9 781646 543243